Piglet and Papa

by Margaret Wild

illustrated by
Stephen Michael King

ABRAMS BOOKS FOR YOUNG READERS
NEW YORK

For Olivia and her dad —M.W.

For Tani —S.M.K.

Library of Congress Cataloging-in-Publication Data:

Wild, Margaret, 1948–
Piglet and Papa / by Margaret Wild ; illustrated by Stephen Michael King.
p. cm.
Summary: When Piglet's beloved father chases her away after she plays too rough, all of the barnyard animals try to make her feel better, but Piglet is still afraid that her father no longer loves her.
ISBN-13: 978-0-8109-1476-6
ISBN-10: 0-8109-1476-X
[1. Father and child—Fiction. 2. Pigs—Fiction. 3. Domestic animals—Fiction. 4. Farm life—Fiction.] I. King, Stephen Michael, ill. II. Title.

PZ7.W64574Pig 2006
[E]—dc22
2006015304

Text copyright © 2007 Margaret Wild
Illustrations copyright © 2007 Stephen Michael King

Book design by Celina Carvalho
Production manager: Alexis Mentor

Printed and bound in Singapore
10 9 8 7 6 5 4 3 2

HNA ▪▪▪▪▪
harry n. abrams, inc.
a subsidiary of La Martinière Groupe
115 West 18th Street
New York, NY 10011
www.hnabooks.com

Piglet loved playing with her papa.

One morning, she
sat on his head,

bounced on
his belly,

and chewed his tail. Hard.

"Ouch!" said Papa. "You little rascal!"
And he chased her out of the sty.

Piglet wasn't sure if he was
really, really cross.
"Do you love me?"
she asked in a small voice,

but Papa was grunting so loudly
he didn't hear.

Piglet crept away.

She saw Horse.

"Hello, Horse," said Piglet.
"Do you love me?"

"I like your cute little ears," said Horse,
"and I do love you—
but someone else loves you
ten times more."

"Who's that?" asked Piglet,
but Horse just smiled
as she swished away the flies.

So Piglet went on her way.

She saw Sheep.

"Hello, Sheep," said Piglet.
"Do you love me?"

"I like your snub little nose," said Sheep,
"and I do love you—
but someone else loves you
a hundred times more."

"Who's that?" asked Piglet,
but Sheep just smiled
as he munched the grass.

So Piglet went on her way.

She saw Donkey.

"Hello, Donkey," said Piglet.
"Do you love me?"

"I like your curly-whirly tail," said Donkey,
"and I do love you—
but someone else loves you
a thousand times more."

"Who's that?" asked Piglet,
but Donkey just smiled
as he kicked up his heels.

So Piglet went on her way.

She saw Duck.

"Hello, Duck," said Piglet.
"Do you love me?"

"I like your little pink trotters," said Duck,
"and I do love you—
but someone else loves you
a million times more."

"Who's that?" asked Piglet,
but Duck just smiled
as she flapped her wings.

So Piglet went on her way.

She saw Dog.

"Hello, Dog," said Piglet.
"Do you love me?"

"I like your fat little tummy," said Dog,
"and I do love you—
but someone else loves you
a billion times more."

"Who's that?" asked Piglet,
but Dog just smiled
as he dug up a bone.

Piglet was tired.
She wanted food and a hug.

So she went back to the sty—
and there was Papa waiting for her.

"Hello, Papa," said Piglet.
"Do you love me?"

"I like your cute little ears," said Papa, "and your snub little nose and your curly-whirly tail and your little pink trotters and your fat little tummy."

"And?" said Piglet.

"And I love you best of all in the whole wide world!"

"I knew *that*!" said Piglet,
and she sat on her papa's head,

bounced on
his belly,

and chewed his tail—
gently.